Communications

Close-up

Radio and

Television

● Communications
Close-up

Radio and Television

IAN GRAHAM

Designer: Simon Borrough
Editors: Nicola Barber, Erik Greb
Illustrations: Richard Morris, Hardlines

Library of Congress Cataloging-in-Publication Data
Graham, Ian.
Radio and Television / Ian Graham.
    p.   cm.–(Communications Close-up)
    Includes index.
    ISBN 0-7398-3187-9
    1. Radio–Juvenile literature.
    2. Television–Juvenile literature.
    [1. Radio. 2. Television.]
    I. Title. II. Series.

Printed in Hong Kong

1 2 3 4 5 6 7 8 9 0 LB 03 02 01 00

Acknowledgments
cover With thanks to Rod Ebdon **page 6** Robert Harding Picture Library **page 7** Press Association/Topham **page 11** Hank Morgan/Science Photo Library **page 12** www.corbis.com/Danny Lehman **page 13** Science Museum/Science and Society Picture Library **page 14** John Edwards/Tony Stone Images **page 15** (top) Janet Gill/Tony Stone Images (bottom) Associated Press/Topham Picture Point **page 20** Jerry Mason/Science Photo Library **page 21** Mr P Clement/Bruce Coleman Limited **page 23** With thanks to Pioneer (left) and Panasonic (right) **page 26** With thanks to Panasonic **page 27** With thanks to Fujifilm **page 28** Michael Rosenfeld/Tony Stone Images **page 29** ©Hank Morgan from Rainbow **page 30** David Joe/Tony Stone Images **page 31** Action-Plus **page 33** Shout/Robert Harding Picture Library **page 34** (top) Alan Levenson/Tony Stone Images (bottom) Alan Wycheck/Tony Stone Images **page 36** www.corbis.com/Jeffrey L.Rotman **page 37** Last Resort Picture Library **page 38** Kathy Bushue/Tony Stone Images **page 39** Michael P Price/Bruce Coleman Limited **page 41** Space Telescope Science Institute/NASA/Science Photo Library

CONTENTS

RADIO WAVES

IF OUR EYES WERE SENSITIVE TO RADIO WAVES, WE WOULD BE DAZZLED BY THE NEVER-ENDING TORRENT OF RADIO ENERGY THAT FLOODS OUR WORLD. WE DEPEND HEAVILY ON RADIO FOR INFORMATION, FOR ENTERTAINMENT, AND FOR SAFETY.

Radio collars enable scientists to track wild animals such as this Siberian tiger. A radio collar sends out signals that allow its location to be plotted.

Radio waves carry radio and television programs into our homes. They carry telephone calls around the world. They link cordless phones to base stations and mobile phones to the telephone network. They relay messages between the emergency services. They carry voice and computer data between Earth and manned spacecraft. Radio signals bring information hundreds of millions of miles from deep space probes, and they allow animals to be tracked through forest and jungle, across the icy polar wastes and into the ocean depths. Modern aviation would be impossible without radio. The radar systems that allow air traffic controllers to guide the world's aircraft safely through the airways all depend on radio waves.

ON STAGE

Radio allows pop stars and television presenters to roam around a stage or studio without having to trail microphone cables behind them. Studio hosts wear a tiny microphone the size of your little fingernail. A fine wire hidden under the clothes connects the microphone to a radio transmitter the size of a pack of playing cards, tucked away in a belt pouch. The signal from the transmitter is picked up by a receiver in the studio and mixed with other microphone signals before transmission. A singer needs to have a microphone very close to his or her lips, so that it picks up only the voice and not the sound of nearby instruments. The singer may carry a radio microphone, or the microphone can be worn on a headset. A thin boom from a head-band holds the microphone immediately in front of the singer's mouth, leaving the hands free. Head-mounted radio microphones allow pop stars to take part in dance routines on stage that would be impossible with a cabled microphone or a handheld radio microphone.

CYBER COPS

A police officer on patrol used to be totally alone. The only way of summoning help was to blow a whistle and hope that someone heard it. Small portable radios revolutionized police work. They enabled police officers to be contacted and to summon help anywhere. Now, some police officers are equipped with computers that are linked to stations by radio, just like their voice radios. The instrument panel of a modern police car can resemble the flight deck of the *Starship Enterprise!* One group of police officers in Dallas, Texas, patrols the city on mountain bikes and keeps in touch with the police station by means of laptop computers with radio links. They can check out people and vehicles by typing the relevant details into their laptop computers.

Radio microphones allow performers to move around the stage without trailing microphone cables behind them. The microphone is connected to a radio transmitter worn on the performer's belt.

History links

DISCOVERING RADIO

In 1873, the Scottish physicist James Clerk Maxwell predicted the existence of radio waves—but he could not prove it. Ten years later, the Irish physicist George Francis Fitzgerald suggested that radio waves could be made by varying an electric current. In 1888, the German scientist Heinrich Hertz demonstrated this and finally proved that Maxwell had been right.

Link-ups

SATELLITE TRACKING

The most advanced radio collars, used for tracking animals, have their own built-in satellite positioning system. Using radio signals from orbiting navigation satellites, the collars determine their position and keep track of the animal they're attached to. Researchers gather information about the animal by sending a coded radio signal to the collar. The signal triggers the collar to transmit details of the animal's movements. These details can be picked up by an aircraft flying up to 15 miles away from the animal. (See pages 38-9 for more about animal tracking.)

WAVES IN THE ETHER

EVERY RADIO COMMUNICATIONS SYSTEM AND TELEVISION BROADCASTING NETWORK DEPENDS ON INVISIBLE WAVES OF ENERGY TRAVELING FROM TRANSMITTER TO RECEIVER. INFORMATION IS ADDED TO THE WAVES BEFORE THEY ARE TRANSMITTED, AND TAKEN OUT AGAIN AFTER THEY ARE RECEIVED.

Radio waves are almost identical to light waves. The only difference is the length of the waves. Light waves are approximately half of one-thousandth of a millimeter long. Radio waves can be anything from a millimeter to hundreds of miles long. They are electromagnetic waves—an electric field and a magnetic field traveling together through space. As the electric field grows, it takes energy from the magnetic field, which shrinks. Then the electric field shrinks and gives energy back to the magnetic field. The two fields hurtle through space at a speed of 186,000 miles per second, constantly exchanging energy between them.

TWO INTO ONE

Radio communications signals are two waves in one. The first is a high-frequency carrier wave. The second is the information that the wave is to carry. The information might be a radio program or a telephone caller's voice. The information wave changes the carrier wave in two possible ways. Changing the size of the carrier wave is called amplitude modulation (AM). Changing its speed of vibration is called frequency modulation (FM). When a receiver picks

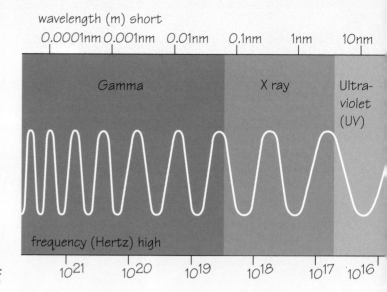

wavelength (m) short

| 0.0001nm | 0.001nm | 0.01nm | 0.1nm | 1nm | 10nm |

Gamma   X ray   Ultra-violet (UV)

frequency (Hertz) high

10^{21} 10^{20} 10^{19} 10^{18} 10^{17} 10^{16}

Radio waves are part of the electromagnetic spectrum, which also includes infrared heat rays, visible light, ultraviolet rays, X rays, and gamma rays. The only difference between them is the length of their waves.

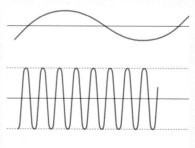

The audio signal

The carrier wave

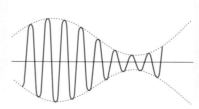

The carrier wave carrying the audio signal by amplitude modulation (AM)

The carrier wave carrying the audio signal by frequency modulation (FM)

A radio signal is made up of two radio waves —a signal representing the information to be carried (top) and a carrier wave (below).

8

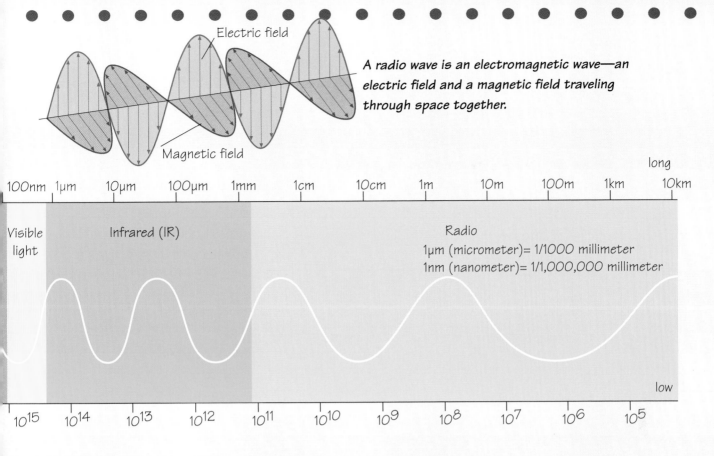

Electric field

Magnetic field

A radio wave is an electromagnetic wave—an electric field and a magnetic field traveling through space together.

| | | | | | | | | | | | long |
| 100nm | 1µm | 10µm | 100µm | 1mm | 1cm | 10cm | 1m | 10m | 100m | 1km | 10km |

Visible light

Infrared (IR)

Radio

1µm (micrometer)= 1/1000 millimeter

1nm (nanometer)= 1/1,000,000 millimeter

low

10^{15} 10^{14} 10^{13} 10^{12} 10^{11} 10^{10} 10^{9} 10^{8} 10^{7} 10^{6} 10^{5}

up the signal, it filters out the carrier wave, leaving the radio program or the telephone caller's voice, which is changed back into sound.

BOUNCING WAVES OFF CLOUDS

Radio waves travel in straight lines, but the Earth is not flat! Because of the Earth's curve, a radio signal transmitted from the top of a 100-meter tower should be able to travel no more than 20 miles at most. In fact, radio signals can be picked up by receivers thousands of miles away, well below the horizon and out of sight of the transmitter. How does this work?

In the same way that light is reflected by clouds of water droplets in the atmosphere, radio waves are reflected by clouds of electrically charged particles. The outer layers of the atmosphere receive enough energy from the Sun to strip electrons away from their atoms, leaving charged particles called ions behind. Radio waves from transmitters on the ground bounce off this layer of ions,

called the ionosphere, and head back down toward the ground. This is how radio broadcasts can travel around the curve of the Earth.

Fortunately, radio waves between about one centimeter and 65 feet long are not reflected by the ionosphere—instead they pass through it. This radio "window" in the atmosphere allows astronomers to pick up natural radio waves from distant stars and galaxies. It also allows scientists to communicate with satellites and spacecraft, and to talk to astronauts on the Moon.

History links

INVENTING RADIO COMMUNICATION

Guglielmo Marconi took out the first patent for "wireless telegraphy" in 1896. By bouncing radio waves off the ionosphere, he sent the first long-distance radio signal across the Atlantic Ocean in 1901.

FLYING BY RADIO

RADIO LINKS AND CLOSED CIRCUIT TELEVISION ALLOW SUBMARINES TO EXPLORE THE OCEAN DEPTHS, SPACECRAFT TO ROAM THE SURFACE OF DISTANT PLANETS, AND JET PLANES TO CLIMB AND DIVE EVEN THOUGH THEIR PILOTS NEVER LEAVE THE GROUND.

The X-36 experimental aircraft sits at the end of a desert runway in California. Its jet engine screams up to full power and the plane accelerates along the runway. Its nose tips up and it soars to a height of more than 3 miles. But there is no pilot on board.

The pilot sits in a virtual cockpit on the ground looking at pictures relayed from a closed circuit television camera in the plane's nose. When the pilot moves the control stick, radio signals carry the information to the plane. A head-up display (HUD), an angled sheet of glass between the pilot and the television screen, shows the pilot vital data, such as air speed and altitude. This data is received by radio from the plane.

The X-36 is only 20 feet long, 10 feet from wing tip to wing tip, and less than 3 feet high—just over one-quarter full size. By taking the pilot out of the plane, this small model can be built and tested much more cheaply than having to build a full-size aircraft with the life-support systems that a pilot would need. It also permits aircraft designers to test their most extreme ideas without risking the life of a pilot. The X-36 was built to test a new design for a future fighter that has no tail. Removing the tail fin makes the plane more agile in dogfights and also more difficult to spot by radar.

The X-36 research plane is flown by a pilot who stays on the ground. A video camera in the plane's nose shows the pilot the view ahead of the plane. The picture and information about the plane are sent to the pilot's cockpit by radio.

Radio link between virtual cockpit and X-36

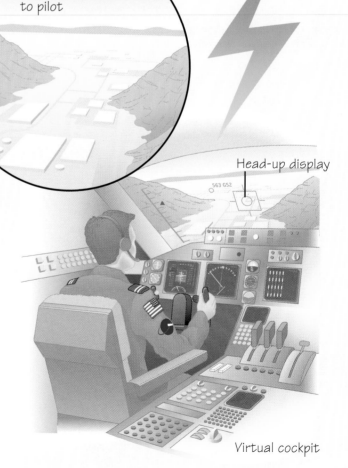

Image from nose camera relayed to pilot

Head-up display

Virtual cockpit

Children in the U.S. talk to a Jason Project diver on the ocean floor off the coast of Belize (see below).

GO FOR A DRIVE ON MARS

When the NASA *Pathfinder* space probe landed on Mars in 1997, it opened up like a flower to reveal the *Sojourner* rover inside. *Sojourner* trundled off the lander and made its way across the sandy, red Martian surface. The rover was driven by a scientist on Earth. Radio signals from the driver took 15 minutes to reach Mars and activate the rover. Pictures from the rover's cameras took another 15 minutes to beam its movements back to Earth. The driver watched the view from the cameras with 3-D glasses to give him the sensation of depth and distance.

VISIT THE BOTTOM OF THE OCEAN

Thousands of school students in classrooms all over the world have looked at live television pictures beamed from a submersible roving around the ocean floor. The pictures appear on the Jason Project's Internet website. Students who go to Jason Project centers at museums in the U.S. and Britain can talk to the scientists at the research site. Scientists elsewhere can use the same system to take part in the project without leaving their laboratories. It is even possible to control the undersea submersibles by satellite from anywhere in the world. Each year, the Jason team explores a different site. Past sites include the Mediterranean Sea, the Great Lakes, the Hawaiian Islands, and Iceland.

History links

LOOKING BACK

Between 1979 and 1983 a supersonic aircraft called HiMAT (Highly Maneuverable Aircraft Technology) explored the limits of fighter agility. It could carry out maneuvers that no human pilot could survive because it was an unmanned radio-controlled aircraft, the forerunner of the X-36.

CABLES AND WAVES

TODAY, RADIO AND TELEVISION PROGRAMS REACH HOMES IN THREE MAIN WAYS—FROM A TRANSMITTER ON THE GROUND, FROM A TRANSMITTER IN SPACE, OR ALONG AN UNDERGROUND CABLE.

Satellite dishes on houses in Mexico. Visit almost any country in the world today and you will see satellite dishes on roof tops. They pick up television programs broadcast by satellites orbiting Earth.

There are more ways of sending and receiving radio and television programs than ever before. A network of transmitters on the ground floods the country with signals that can be picked up by rooftop antennas or small antennas attached to portable radio and television sets. Satellites beam signals straight down to dish antennas. Underground fiber optic cables carry not only radio and television programs but also telephone services.

TWO-WAY TALK

The signals for ground-based and satellite television travel through the system in one direction only—from the transmitter on the ground or in space to the antenna that picks them up. A cable network allows two-way communication. This means that the television set has become interactive. By punching numbers on a remote control handset, you can buy a pay-per-view broadcast, such as a movie, a sports event, or a rock concert.

Many cable television companies offer a service called Near Video On Demand. They transmit the same film again and again throughout the day, a different film on each channel. You pay to watch the next available transmission by punching a unique code number into a handset. The number whizzes down the fiber optic cable to the company's computer, which allows your cable decoder to access the film. It also automatically adds the pay-per-view charge to your bill.

THE LONG AND SHORT OF IT

The only difference between the radio waves used for communications, radio broadcasting, and television broadcasting is the length of the waves—the wavelength. The shortest radio waves are reserved for satellite broadcasts. There are two reasons for this. First, long-wave signals need large antennas to pick them up, while short waves can be picked up by a smaller antenna. There isn't much room on a satellite for antennas, so small antennas are better. Second, the higher the frequency (speed of vibration) of a radio signal, the more information it can carry. High-frequency signals have short wavelengths. Television signals have to carry a lot of information, so they are broadcast using a very high-frequency signal. Satellites use radio signals with frequencies between four and 30 gigahertz. One

gigahertz is one billion hertz (vibrations) per second.

Ground-based, or terrestrial, transmitters broadcast television programs at lower frequencies, anything from 45MHz to 900MHz (MHz means one million hertz). At these frequencies, the radio waves are between about 20 feet and 1 foot long.

Radio programs and voice communications do not contain as much information as television programs, so they can be broadcast using lower frequencies with longer wavelengths. A typical FM music station is broadcast at about 100MHz with a wavelength of 10 feet. However, AM radio stations are broadcast at lower frequencies, using waves between a couple of hundred and a couple of thousand feet long, with poorer sound quality.

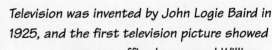

History links

THE FIRST TELEVISION SET

The first experiment in transmitting television pictures by cable took place in the United States in 1927. Cable television spread rapidly nationwide in the 1960s. The copper cables used in these early cable systems are now being replaced by fiber optic cables.

Television was invented by John Logie Baird in 1925, and the first television picture showed an office boy named William Taynton. Baird's television was mechanical (left), but when the BBC began the world's first regular television broadcasts in England in 1936, they used a new electronic television system invented by the British electronics company EMI.

ON GIANTS' SHOULDERS

If you want to see a long way, you have to climb to a high place. If you want a radio signal to travel a long way, the transmitter has to be placed as high as possible. That is why radio transmitters are usually perched on top of tall towers. Some of the tallest structures on Earth are communications towers.

As some cities have attracted more businesses and become more prosperous, their skylines have changed. Skyscrapers have sprung up everywhere. Unfortunately, these tall buildings block radio signals. So, radio transmitters have also had to be raised up on tall towers. Communications towers handle two types of radio signals: microwaves and broadcast signals. Microwaves travel as thin beams in straight lines from one point to another. This means that the two microwave antennas have to be pointed very accurately at each other. Microwaves are used to send radio and TV programs from studios to a transmitter, or to relay telephone calls across the country. Broadcast signals travel outward in all directions, sending radio and television programs to a wide area around the tower.

TALLEST OF THE TALL

One of the world's tallest buildings is the CN Tower (left), a communications tower in Toronto, Canada. It stands about 1,815 feet high. There are microwave receivers housed in a doughnut-shaped structure, 1,000 feet from the ground. They pick up distant signals and relay them to the transmission antenna that tops the tower. This antenna broadcasts 16 television and FM radio signals across southern Ontario.

Even though the tower weighs an incredible 118,000 tons and its hollow structure makes it immensely strong, it still moves in the wind. The tip of the antenna can sway more than 6 feet away from the tower's center-line in strong winds. The Sky Pod below it, which is open to tourists, can sway up to 3 feet.

TOWERING OVER LONDON

At 620 feet, the BT Tower in London is a pygmy compared to the CN Tower! It has more than 50 microwave dishes, relaying television programs, live outside broadcasts, telephone conversations, and computer data to other towers situated around London.

All of Britain's television broadcasters and some American broadcasters rely on the BT Tower to relay programs to transmitters on the ground and in space. Signals bound for television satellites are sent to the tower, which relays them by microwave to the London Teleport (one of BT's ground stations) for onward transmission up to the satellites.

Dozens of microwave dishes at the top of London's BT Tower relay telephone calls and broadcasts to other towers around the capital.

GETTING TO THE BOTTOM OF IT

As shown by that famous leaning tower in Pisa, Italy, a tall structure has to be built on firm foundations. The taller and thinner the tower, the more critical are the foundations. More than 50,000 tons of rock were excavated to install the CN Tower's foundations. They do their job perfectly, but the tower still leans by a couple of inches because of the effect of Earth's spin on a structure of that height in that part of the world. The builders of the BT Tower in London faced a different problem. The tower had to be built on soft London clay. The solution was to lay a concrete raft 88 feet square by 3 feet thick, 26 feet below ground level. A flat-topped concrete pyramid 23 feet tall was built on top of the raft and the tower was built on top of the pyramid.

History links

AN UNSCHEDULED LANDING

On July 28, 1945, the Empire State building (right), then the world's tallest building, was swathed in clouds. The pilot of a B25 bomber flying over New York failed to see the building, and the plane smashed straight into it. The plane's wings were torn off, one engine fell down an elevator shaft, and the other flew right through the building and out the other side. Today, all of the world's tallest skyscrapers and communications towers are equipped with high-intensity flashing warning lights so that they can be seen easily by pilots.

BROADCASTING SATELLITES

THE HIGHER A BROADCASTING TRANSMITTER IS, THE BETTER, BECAUSE ITS SIGNALS REACH FARTHER. THE BEST TRANSMITTERS ARE SO HIGH THAT THEY ARE ABOVE EARTH'S ATMOSPHERE ALTOGETHER. SATELLITES CAN NOW BROADCAST TELEVISION AND RADIO PROGRAMS DIRECTLY INTO OUR HOMES FROM SPACE.

Dozens of television satellites circle the world, beaming television and radio programs down to millions of people on Earth. Broadcasters transmit programs up to the satellite. The satellite receives them, amplifies them, shifts them down in frequency, and retransmits them down to receiving dishes on Earth. The signal beamed up to the satellite is called the uplink and the signal sent back down to Earth is the downlink. The receiving dishes on Earth might be large dishes belonging to cable television companies, which then distribute the signals to their subscribers, or they might be small dishes attached to individual houses. One satellite can cover a whole country—or several countries—replacing hundreds, possibly thousands, of transmitters and relay stations on the ground.

Broadcasting satellite

22,000 mi

Downlink

Uplink

The area on the ground covered by a signal beamed down to Earth from a television satellite in orbit is called the satellite's "footprint."

Downlink

Footprint

16

INSIDE A SATELLITE

A typical television satellite has four parts—the main structure, the electronics payload, the propulsion system, and the electrical power system. The main structure is a strong metal frame to which all the other parts of the satellite are attached. It has to be strong enough to hold the satellite together through the stresses and vibration of launch. The electronics payload includes all the radio equipment, the antennas and the amplifiers. They are surrounded by shiny metal foil to reflect sunlight, so that they don't overheat.

The satellite's propulsion system includes a large rocket motor, and the apogee kick motor, which moves it into the correct orbit after launch. The satellite is kept in precisely the right position by puffs of hydrazine gas from thrusters controlled from Earth. A satellite usually carries about ten years' supply of hydrazine.

Electrical power for the electronics and radio equipment is produced by solar panels which convert sunlight directly into electricity. A typical television broadcasting satellite generates between 5,000 and 10,000 watts of electricity in this way. When the satellite is shaded by Earth and the solar panels stop working, batteries take over. The solar panels keep the batteries fully charged.

SATELLITE RADIO

Satellite television has been so successful that radio broadcasters are lining up to distribute their services by satellite. Satellite radio broadcasting is particularly effective in the developing world, where it is impossible to cover the whole countryside with ground transmitters. In the near future, the WorldSpace satellite network will make near CD-quality radio broadcasts available to more than four billion people in Africa, the Middle East, Asia, and Latin America. The low-cost portable radio sets designed to be used with the satellites will also receive normal radio programs from ground transmitters.

The solar panels on a broadcasting satellite generate electricity for its on-board radio equipment, while its antennas are kept pointing at Earth.

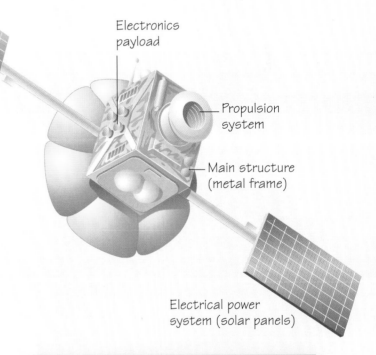

Electronics payload

Propulsion system

Main structure (metal frame)

Electrical power system (solar panels)

History links

THE TV ORBIT

Television satellites are strung out along a special orbit 22,000 miles above Earth's equator. At that distance, they orbit at the same speed as the Earth turns, so they stay in the same spot in the sky, 24 hours a day. This orbit, geostationary orbit, is now very crowded, with more than 200 satellites in place. Each new satellite is allocated a position, or orbital slot, by international agreement.

PACKING THE AIRWAVES

WE ARE USING RADIO WAVES MORE THAN EVER BEFORE, AND THE DEMAND FOR NEW FREQUENCIES INCREASES ALL THE TIME. THERE ARE ONLY A LIMITED NUMBER OF FREQUENCIES FOR ALL OF THESE NEW RADIO SIGNALS, SO ENGINEERS ARE DEVELOPING WAYS OF PACKING MORE RADIO SIGNALS INTO THE SAME FREQUENCIES TO SATISFY THE SOARING DEMAND FOR RADIO COMMUNICATION.

There is such a great demand for radio communications that it doesn't make sense to waste time transmitting nothing. Yet that is precisely what happens. The radio spectrum, the tuning scale on a radio set, is divided into a series of different frequencies. Each transmitted signal has its own frequency, and if nothing is being transmitted on that frequency, it lies silent and unused. It's like sending hundreds of cars from one place to another by giving each one its own highway. Most of the road space will be empty most of the time. It would be much more efficient to send all of the cars down one highway. Radio engineers are developing ways of doing the same thing with radio traffic.

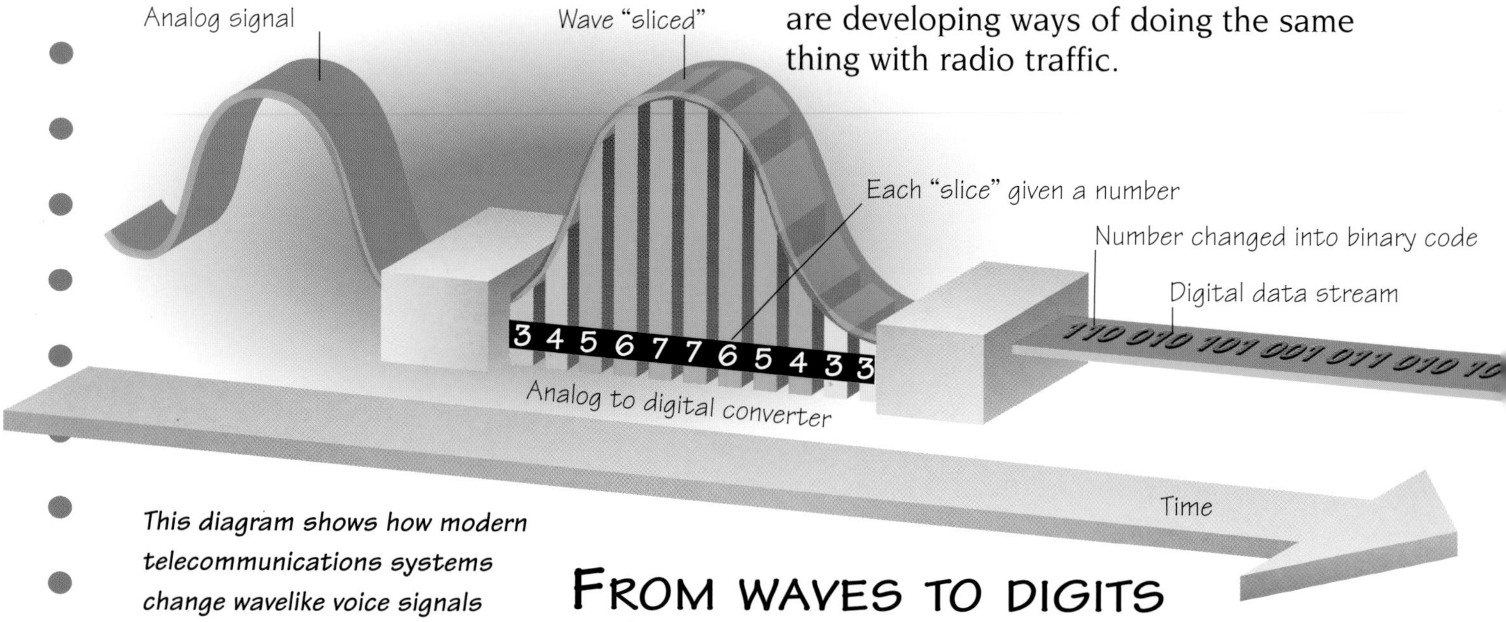

Analog signal

Wave "sliced"

Each "slice" given a number

Number changed into binary code

Digital data stream

3 4 5 6 7 7 6 5 4 3 3

Analog to digital converter

Time

This diagram shows how modern telecommunications systems change wavelike voice signals into a stream of zeroes and ones, called binary code, so that they can be processed by computers. Not only can digital signals be processed at high speed by computers, they are also better at surviving damage from interference.

FROM WAVES TO DIGITS

Modern radio communications systems increasingly use digital signals. All the signals start off as analog waves. These waves are a copy of the sound that is to be transmitted. They are changed from waves to digits by a process called sampling. About 8,000 times a second, the size of the analog wave is measured (sampled) and changed into a number. Each number is then changed into ones and zeroes, at the rate of 64,000 per second. This huge number is often reduced to something more manageable before the signal is transmitted by a mathematical process called compression.

Digital technology makes it possible to chop radio signals up into tiny chunks for transmission and put them back together again when they are received. Chunks of different messages can be packed tightly together so that none of the precious radio spectrum is wasted. One way of doing this is to give each signal its own series of time slots, each lasting a tiny fraction of a second. In the spaces between these time slots, other signals are sent in their own time slots. Thus, lots of different signals can be sent on one frequency. This is called Time Division Multiple Access (TDMA).

FREQUENCY HOPPING

A lot more signals can be sent by chopping the signals up into even smaller chunks and sending them over a band of different frequencies. This means that lots of signals can share a band of frequencies very efficiently, with the minimum of waste. Each chunk of signal has a unique code so that a receiver can recognize which chunks belong to the same message and which it should ignore. Chopping up radio signals and sending them over lots of different frequencies is called spread spectrum radio, frequency hopping, or Code Division Multiple Access (CDMA).

History links

HOPPING ALL THE WAY FROM HOLLYWOOD

Frequency hopping radio communication was invented by the Hollywood actress Hedy Lamarr and the composer George Antheil in 1941 as a way of sending secret radio messages from a submarine.

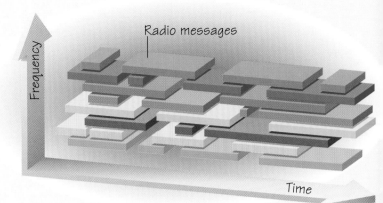

The simplest way of letting lots of people communicate at the same time is to give each radio message a different frequency.

Another way of transmitting lots of messages at the same time is to slice the messages up and give each slice its own time slot (TDMA).

Advanced communications systems split radio messages into tiny chunks, which are spread over all the available frequencies (CDMA).

CLOSED CIRCUIT TELEVISION

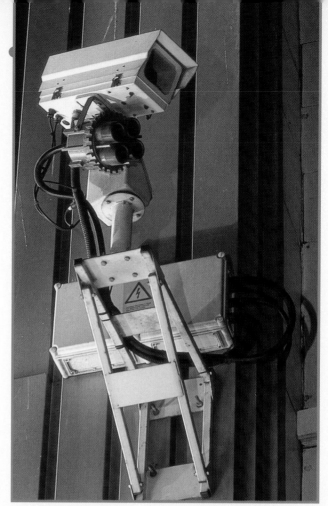

CLOSED CIRCUIT TELEVISION (CCTV) SENDS PICTURES FROM VIDEO CAMERAS TO ONE PARTICULAR VIDEO SCREEN, OR SEVERAL VIDEO SCREENS, INSTEAD OF BROADCASTING THEM. CCTV ACTS AS A REMOTE ELECTRONIC EYE IN PLACES THAT ARE DIFFICULT TO MONITOR.

CCTV cameras are becoming an increasingly common sight in public places such as parking lots and shopping malls, where they provide extra security for shoppers and workers.

The next time you're out shopping, see how many video cameras you can spot. Stores and shopping malls use video cameras to identify thieves. Office doorways are watched by video cameras to monitor people as they come and go. Cameras look down on busy highways and intersections to give an early warning of traffic problems. CCTV has lots of other uses, from wildlife filming and inspecting sewers to bomb disposal and the movie business.

UNCHARTED TERRITORY

Remote video cameras can explore places where people can't go. Problems in underground ducts, pipe conduits, and drains are sometimes diagnosed by feeding a video camera through to relay a picture of the problem to a screen on the surface. Cameras also venture into places that are too dangerous for people. Bomb disposal teams often send robots equipped with video cameras to film suspect devices, vehicles, and buildings before the bomb disposal experts go in. Dogs wearing video cameras have been trained to enter buildings where dangerous people may be hiding. As the dog goes through the building, the agents outside see a "dog's-eye" view of the rooms, helping them to assess the situation.

MAKING MOVIES

When the great movies of the past were made, the only person who knew precisely how each scene had been filmed was the camera operator whose eye was pressed against the camera's viewfinder. The director had to wait until the film had been developed to see it. By then, it was often too late to go back and re-shoot a scene. Now, the camera's viewfinder feeds a video image of the action to a video monitor on the set.

The director can watch the scene and see the same view as the camera operator. The director can assess each scene as it is being filmed and re-shoot it, if necessary, immediately.

TRACKING TRAFFIC

Video cameras perch on top of tall towers overlooking busy roads. If you spot one of these cameras and watch it for a time, you may notice it moving. Pictures from all the cameras along one section of highway are fed to video screens in a control room. Operators in the control room can turn and tilt the cameras by moving a joystick. They can also make a camera zoom in to show a close-up of a small part of the view.

The cameras are difficult to get at for repairs, so they have to work reliably in all weather. A water-resistant housing keeps rain out of the electronics. A sunshield reduces glare and stops rain or snow from settling on the faceplate in front of the lens. Some cameras have heaters that switch on automatically in cold weather.

History links

THE DEVELOPMENT OF VIDEO RECORDING

The first video tape recorder to go on sale was made by the Ampex Corporation in the United States in 1956. Portable home video cameras and recorders were introduced by Sony in 1965. Until then, the only way to make a home video recording outdoors was to connect a video camera to a fixed video recorder by a long cable. In 1976, JVC introduced the Video Home System (VHS), which became the world's favorite home-video tape format. As the technology improves, each new video format is smaller than the last. The first video tape recording machines used video tape 50 millimeters wide. Today's Video 8 format uses video tape only eight millimeters wide.

WILD PICTURES

Video cameras reveal the normally hidden worlds of animal burrows, insect nests, and birds' nests. However, there are still times when it's too dark even for the most modern video camera. Artificial lights are often used, because animals are surprisingly tolerant of bright lights in their normally dark homes. Outside, where larger animals avoid bright lights, image intensifiers and even heat-sensitive, infrared cameras record the activities of timid nocturnal creatures.

A bank vole hoards apples in its underground run, unaware that it is being observed by a tiny camera hidden in the run.

DIGITAL VERSATILE DISKS

TODAY, VIDEO RECORDING MEANS USING VIDEO CASSETTES. WITHIN A COUPLE OF YEARS, THE DIGITAL REVOLUTION WILL TRANSFORM HOME VIDEO. WE WILL BE MAKING DIGITAL VIDEO RECORDINGS ON MINI VIDEO DISKS WITH FAR BETTER PICTURE AND SOUND QUALITY.

The future of the compact disk is here already, and it's also the future of digital video. It is DVD—the Digital Versatile Disk. The disk is the same size as a CD, 5 inches across, but it can hold a lot more information. A standard audio CD can hold about 600 megabytes (600 million bytes) of digital information, equivalent to about an hour of music. Video and audio information can be stored on a DVD in lots of different ways—which is why it's called a versatile disk.

A DVD can hold at least 4.7 gigabytes (4.7 billion bytes) of information. One disk can store a whole movie with picture quality far better than the older, bigger 12-inch laser disks. There is enough space left on the disk to store the soundtrack in two ways. Movies on DVD will have a stereo soundtrack with CD sound-quality or better. In addition, most movies on DVD will also have the same soundtrack recorded on six different sound channels, just like the six-channel soundtrack played in the movie theater. Two channels provide the standard left and right stereo sounds. The third channel provides sounds that seem to come from the center of the screen, including most of the spoken dialogue. Two more channels, called surround channels, send sound-effects

Some DVDs double their playing time by having two recordings on the same side. The recordings are stored on two different layers 40 thousandths of a millimeter apart.

Top layer

The laser beam automatically refocuses to switch between layers

Bottom layer

Some DVDs have two layers

to loudspeakers behind the viewer. The final channel supplies low-frequency, rumbling, bass sounds to a subwoofer loudspeaker. There is only one subwoofer channel, because the sounds are so low that the listener can't tell which direction they're coming from.

Since any information that can be digitized can be stored on a DVD, there will be other forms of DVD. The DVD-ROM, for example, is the DVD version of the CD-ROM, for storing computer data. The first computers with built-in DVD-ROM drives are already in the stores. Recordable disks and DVD recorders have been developed, too.

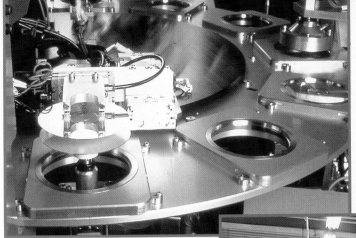

A row of brand new DVD players take their positions at the test station (below). Racks of test gear automatically check the operation of the player's laser, its disk tracking mechanism, and electronics.

DVDs are manufactured in the same way as CDs (above). Much of the manufacturing process is automated. The disks are carried along the production line, from one work station to the next, as the various layers are deposited and built up. The disks are manufactured in rooms that are kept as clean as hospital operating rooms.

GETTING MORE DATA ON THE DISK

Scientists are already developing laser disks that can store even more information than a DVD. Up to now, all laser disk systems have used red or infrared laser beams to read information on the disk. DVD uses a red laser with a finer, brighter and sharper beam than ever before. Blue lasers, which are more difficult to make, increase the amount of information a DVD can hold. The shorter wavelength blue light enables disk makers to boost the disk to a massive 11.8 gigabytes. They are aiming to reach at least 15 gigabytes—25 times the amount of information stored on a standard CD today.

History links

LASERS AND DISKS

The first laser was built by Theodore Maiman in the United States in 1960. The first video disk read by laser, called LaserVision, was introduced by Philips in 1972. The audio compact disk, or CD, was developed jointly by Sony and Philips, and introduced in 1982.

Link-ups

MINI-DVD

Pocket versions of DVDs and DVD players and recorders are being developed. The mini-DVD will be 3 inches across and will hold 1.4 gigabytes of data on one side—more than double a standard CD today. There is already a miniature recordable digital laser disk, called MiniDisc. The tiny disk, only 2.5 inches across, can hold more than an hour of high-quality music. Its inventor, Sony, and Fujitsu, have joined forces to develop a high density MiniDisc that will rival the 3-inch mini-DVD in portable audio. Future camcorders will use these tiny disks, too, instead of bulky tape cassettes.

DIGITAL BROADCASTING

ONE OF THE MOST IMPORTANT DEVELOPMENTS IN RADIO TECHNOLOGY IS THE CHANGE FROM ANALOG TO DIGITAL BROADCASTING. DIGITAL BROADCASTING IS BRINGING BETTER-QUALITY SOUND AND PICTURES, AND IS TURNING OUR TELEVISION SETS INTO COMPUTERS.

One of the three ways of receiving digital television signals is via a satellite dish.

Digital television can be received through an ordinary rooftop television antenna.

Cable television companies can supply digital television through fiber optic cables.

A decoder changes the digital signals so that a television set can use them.

Radio and television programs have been broadcast in the same way for the past 50 years. There have been some improvements, but engineers are now developing a new system that is capable of producing even better-quality pictures.

Since broadcasting began, radio and television programs have been broadcast by analog radio waves. Although this method works reasonably well most of the time, the waves can be damaged and distorted by reflections and interference from other radio waves. When analog waves are damaged or distorted, some of the information they are carrying is lost. However, digital signals are much better at surviving interference.

A digital radio signal is made from waves but, unlike an analog radio signal, the waves represent a code (see page 18). Even if a digital signal is damaged or distorted by interference, sound and picture quality don't suffer—as long as the receiver can detect the code in the signal. So digital radio and television broadcasts give much better sound and picture quality than analog broadcasts.

The TV viewer operates the TV set and decoder by remote control.

SQUEEZING THE BITS

High-quality digital pictures contain about five times as much information as ordinary television pictures. To transmit them, the digital code would have to be sent at the rate of a billion bits of information per second. But a standard television channel can manage only 20 million bits per second. Fortunately, the code can be reduced by a process called data compression so that it fits into a standard television channel. Data compression is so efficient that the channel carries not only better-quality pictures, but also multi-channel, CD-quality sound. It is possible for a film to be broadcast with several soundtracks in different languages. The viewer would choose a particular language from an on-screen menu by pressing buttons on the remote control.

For interactive services the TV set will link service providers by cable or telephone.

A computer center relays two-way links between viewers and interactive service providers.

Signals from viewers will be transmitted back to broadcasters during interactive TV programs.

Home shopping will permit people to order anything from CDs to a new car or their groceries.

It will be possible to access the Internet through your TV set as easily as using a computer today.

Home banking will allow viewers to pay bills from their bank accounts by using their TV sets.

MAKING THE CHANGE

The main disadvantage of digital television is that the millions of television sets already in use cannot pick up digital broadcasts. The sets we watch today are designed to pick up analog signals. But by plugging in a digital decoder box, they can be adapted to receive digital broadcasts. In a few years, many people will be watching digital television and listening to digital radio. Some time in the future, the analog broadcasts that we all listen to and watch today will be switched off for good.

Link-ups

DIGITAL ICE

In-car entertainment (ICE) is big business today. ICE systems include radios, cassette players, CD players, high-power amplifiers, and high-quality loudspeakers. You can buy a digital radio for a car, but at the moment these radios are too big to fit into a car's instrument panel. Instead, the bulky electronics have to be put in the car's trunk. They are also extremely expensive. But, as with all other electrical appliances, the electronics will be miniaturized and the price will drop until everyone has digital radios in their cars.

21st-Century Screens

Television screens have used the same technology since they were invented just over 100 years ago. But increasing demand for larger television screens is encouraging scientists to develop new screen technologies for the 21st century.

A television screen is the front of a large glass tube, a cathode ray tube. Electrons fired from guns at the back of the tube trace out a pattern of lines across the screen. The back of the screen is coated with chemicals called phosphors, which glow when electrons hit them, forming the television picture.

Larger television screens are popular today, but if they get any bigger, the television tube will be too big to get through a normal door and so heavy that it would have to be moved by a forklift! The technology is available to produce lightweight flat television screens more than a yard across. But prices are astronomical—more than $10,000 for one screen! Scientists are racing to develop inexpensive flat, thin TV screens.

Television screens are changing in two ways. The latest TV sets have wider screens. New materials and technologies also make it possible to build very thin, flat screens.

Flat facts

There are dozens of ways to make a thin, flat screen. Two new technologies seem to be the most promising—the plasma display panel and the electroluminescent display.

A plasma display panel works like millions of minute fluorescent lights. Gas inside the display is charged by electricity applied to metal grids at the back and front of the display. The charged gas gives off invisible ultraviolet energy. Phosphors inside the display absorb this energy and glow red, green, or blue. An electroluminescent display is made from a thin film of phosphor sandwiched between two panels. The panels are electrical insulators. When voltage is applied from one panel to the other, electrons are released inside the display. They strike the phosphors, which glow.

Another technology being investigated is based on the type of liquid crystal display used in portable computers and digital watches. Yet another type of screen, the field emission display, uses the fact that electrons can be made to spray away from sharp points. A field emission display is a flat plate covered with microscopic metal points. The points spray electrons onto phosphors, which glow. Scientists have discovered that they can produce the same effect by printing the electrodes on the glass using a cheap method similar to inkjet printing.

GETTING IT ALL TO WORK

One of the stumbling blocks preventing these new types of displays from being built into television sets is the incredibly complicated electronics needed to make them work. A standard TV screen has just two main screen controls—one moves the electron beams across the screen, while the other moves the beams down the screen. But in the new flat screens, each one of the screen's millions of points of light has to be controlled separately, switching on and off dozens of times each second. Just a few years ago, it would have been inconceivable to build this level of computing power into an ordinary television set. But what was impossible a few years ago is merely difficult now. Tomorrow, it may be commonplace.

WIDESCREEN TV

Digital television screens and pictures are a different shape from the TV pictures that we're used to. Standard television sets have screens with a shape that is four units wide by three units high. Digital television sets have screens that are 16 units wide and nine units high – perfect for showing widescreen films. Television programs are now being made with this frame format.

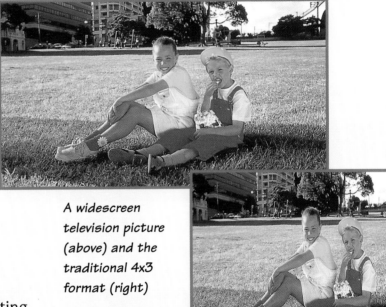

A widescreen television picture (above) and the traditional 4x3 format (right)

History links

THE CATHODE RAY TUBE

The cathode ray tube (CRT), the device that became the television picture tube that we still use today, was invented in 1897 by Ferdinand Braun. His first CRT produced a glowing dot which could be moved around on a screen. "Cathode ray" is another name for a stream of electrons (tiny particles of matter with a negative electric charge) coming from a negative electrode, which is also called a cathode.

ROBOT VISION

ROBOTS "SEE" THROUGH VIDEO-CAMERA EYES. THE SIMPLEST ROBOT CAMERAS SHOW A HUMAN OPERATOR THE VIEW FROM THE ROBOT, BUT SCIENTISTS ARE TRYING TO DEVELOP ROBOTS THAT CAN "UNDERSTAND" WHAT THEIR TV-CAMERA EYES SEE.

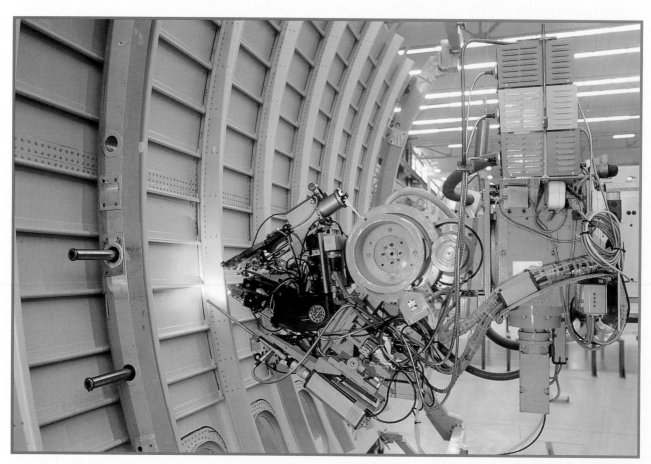

An industrial robot works on the main fuselage of an Airbus airliner. Industrial robots can do the same job over and over again to the same high standard without breaks or vacations.

Sight is a clever trick. For all their gigabytes of memory and hundreds of megahertz of processing speed, computers and robots cannot yet compete with the human eye. Robots look out on the world with video-camera eyes, but their computer brain has great difficulty understanding what they are looking at. Scientists have been trying for years to build robot vision systems, but progress has been very slow. However, a new type of computer that mimics the way the human brain works might achieve more success.

TOWARD TOMORROW

Scientists at the Massachusetts Institute of Technology are developing a robot called Kismet which they hope will eventually be more humanlike than any robot to date. Kismet has been given the communication skills of a baby. It changes its facial expression depending on whether it sees a face or an inanimate object in front of it. It shows interest in nearby movements and can show fear if the movements become too fast and frantic. If it is left alone for too long, it starts to look sad. Kismet is just the first stage of a project called Cog to make an intelligent artificial being. Kismet responds to its surroundings, but it doesn't understand what it sees through its human-looking eyes.

GIVING ROBOTS SIGHT

If future robots are to respond in a truly humanlike way, they will have to be able to understand what they see. They will need a computerized brain of some sort. If it is not possible to build all the necessary computing power into the robot, its "brain" could be somewhere else, linked to the robot by radio.

The modern-day computers used by most people work in a completely different way from the human brain. computers process information piece by piece, one piece after another. In the human brain, information is split up into lots of different pieces that are processed in different parts of the brain at the same time. However, scientists are developing a new type of computer, called a neural net, which works more like the brain—by processing different parts of a problem at the same time.

Inside the human brain, each brain cell

INVENTING ROBOTS

The word "robot" was invented in 1921 by the Czech playwright Karel Capek, to describe mechanical people in his play R.U.R.

makes lots of connections to the other brain cells surrounding it. There are millions upon millions of these connections inside the human brain. Neural nets copy the brain's structure by being stacked on top of each other, with lots of connections between them. When these layered neural nets process visual information, they may be able to produce the sensation that we call sight.

One way of making layered neural nets is to stack neural net chips on top of each other and interconnect them with wires or laser beams. A better way is to make ultra-thin processors. These processors are so thin that electrons, the particles that carry information around a computer, can actually pass between the layers. Thousands of processors can be built on a single chip. Scientists researching these extraordinary neural computers say that they do appear to behave like brain cells. In the near future, a primitive robot brain made from these processors is scheduled to be switched on so that it can start learning from its environment.

Robots have to sense the world around them. Video cameras serve as eyes and fingertip sensors ensure that a robot's hand grips only as tightly as it needs to.

DISTANCE READING

RADIO LINKS ENABLE US TO RECEIVE INFORMATION THAT IS A LONG WAY AWAY. SENSORS COLLECT INFORMATION FROM DISTANT RACE CARS, ROCKETS, OR SPACECRAFT AND SEND IT BY RADIO TO A DIFFERENT PLACE TO BE ANALYZED.

Taking measurements or collecting data in one place and sending the information to another place is called "telemetry," from Greek words meaning "measuring at a distance." Telemetry gives scientists and engineers vital information about how well all sorts of machines, electronic systems, and even the human body are working. It often provides early warning of problems, so that scientists, engineers, or doctors can fix them more quickly and efficiently.

A patient receives emergency treatment. Precious time can be saved by sending test results ahead by radio from the patient's home or an ambulance.

MEDICAL TELEMETRY

Remote monitoring is especially valuable in medicine. A patient suffering from a suspected heart attack can have the results of an electrocardiogram (a trace of the heart's electrical activity) taken in their home or in an ambulance. The information is sent ahead by radio to the hospital so that a doctor watching the trace can assess the patient's heart problem before he or she arrives at the hospital. Any necessary specialist treatment or surgery can be organized and prepared before the patient arrives.

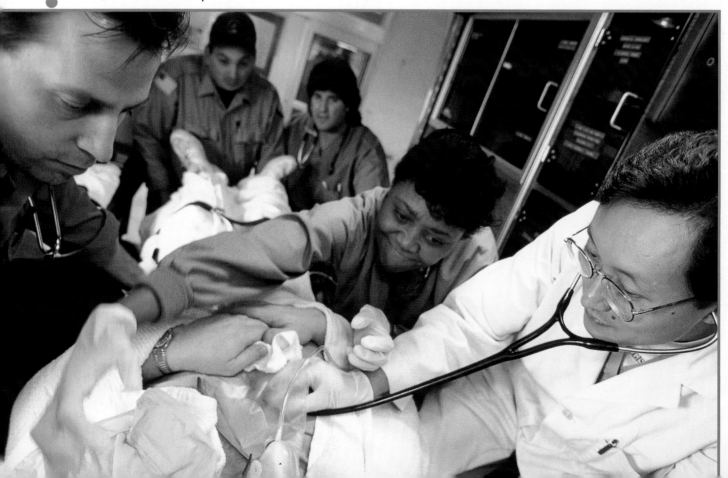

EARLY WARNING

Telemetry, or remote monitoring, can detect problems or faults in a machine long before the senses pick them up. As a rocket rises from its launchpad on a plume of flame, sensors monitor its course, the state of its fuel tanks, and the performance of its engines. If it deviates from its planned course, or any part of the rocket breaks down, the launch safety officer can see the problem immediately on a computer screen and make an instant decision either to allow the rocket to continue—or to destroy it safely.

SPACE MEDICINE

Telemetry enables doctors to monitor Space Shuttle astronauts during a flight. Before launch, the astronauts have three electrodes attached to them—two on the chest and one on the head. These electrodes pick up the heart's electrical activity which is relayed to the flight surgeon on Earth. The system enables space mission planners to change a mission plan if the astronauts need more rest, or if they can do more work than expected. It also helps planners to design future space missions to keep astronauts healthy, alert, and working at their best.

History links

SPACE DATA

The first U.S. astronaut, Alan Shepard, was fitted with sensors that measured his respiration (breathing), temperature, and heart rate. A blood pressure sensor was developed for later flights. At liftoff, telemetry showed his heart-rate soaring to 126 beats per minute and his breathing quickening to 40 breaths per minute.

Link-ups

HEART ALARM

The University of Tokyo has developed a sensor to help heart attack and stroke sufferers. A stroke is a sudden interruption in the blood supply to part of the brain, caused by blocked or leaking blood vessels. Electrodes attached to the patient's body monitor the heart's electrical activity, while other instruments monitor the patient's body movements. The information is relayed to a nearby computer which automatically telephones an alarm signal to the hospital if the patient collapses with a heart attack or stroke.

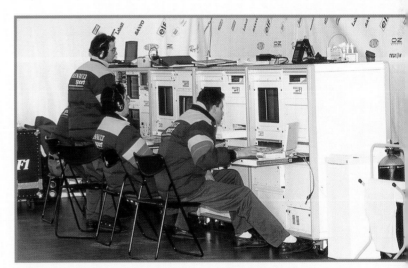

Formula One race car engineers monitor data arriving by radio from their car on the track.

RACING FOR DATA

A modern Formula 1 race car contains more than a half mile of electric cable linked to a hundred sensors and other instruments. On every lap of a race, the car's on-board radio transmitter sends out about 20 megabytes of data which are picked up by the team's computers at the trackside. If engineers spot the slightest deviation from peak performance, they can talk to the driver by radio and tell him what they think is wrong and whether a pit stop is needed to repair it.

RADAR

RADIO WAVES ARE USEFUL TOOLS FOR PROBING THE WORLD AROUND US. THEY CAN SHOW WHERE SOMETHING IS, HOW FAR AWAY IT IS, HOW FAST IT IS TRAVELING, AND IN WHICH DIRECTION IT IS MOVING.

If you bounce a ball off a wall, it comes back to you. Bounce it against a wall that's farther away and it takes longer to come back. The time it takes for the ball to bounce back shows how far away the wall is. You can do the same thing with radio waves. Bouncing radio waves off things to learn about where they are and how they are moving is called radio detection and ranging, or radar. Radio waves travel at the speed of light so they bounce back much faster than a ball hitting a wall, and they can measure the distance to far-away objects very quickly.

The Doppler Effect and Doppler Shift were named after the scientist who first studied and described them in 1842— Christian Doppler (1805-53).

As the car races away, radio waves reflected by it are spread out.

Radio waves reflected by an approaching car are bunched up closer together

SPEED CHECK
Radar can measure speed as well as distance. One application is the

A policeman uses a radar gun to catch speeding motorists.

radar speed trap. A radar gun fires radio waves at a car. The waves hit the car at the speed of light and bounce back to a receiver in the gun. If the car is racing away from the gun, the radio waves that bounce back from it are longer than the waves sent out by the gun. If the car is racing toward the gun, the reflected waves are shorter. By measuring how much the waves have been shortened or lengthened, the gun can work out how fast the car is going. Speeding drivers beware!

HOME SECURITY

Many homes now have their own radar systems. The main living room of a house is often protected by a motion detector. If anything in the room moves, an alarm sounds. Movement in the room is detected by a mini-radar set using microwave radio waves. If a microwave detector alone is used, any motion can set the system off, for example, a curtain blowing in the breeze or a magazine sliding off a table. So the microwave detector usually works together with a second detector, an infrared detector, which responds to heat sources in the room. A hot spot on a table caused by sunlight shining through a window is picked up by the infrared detector but not by the microwave detector. The alarm sounds only if both detectors are triggered. The heat and movement of a burglar walking across the room are picked up by both detectors, which trigger the alarm.

STORM SCIENCE

Radar can measure the speed of wind by bouncing radio waves off particles and other debris blown by the wind. In October 1998, when Hurricane Georges came ashore in Florida, two especially reinforced trucks full of scientific instruments were waiting for it. Inside the trucks was mobile radar equipment designed to measure the hurricane's wind speed at certain points. Scientists believe that tongues of particularly strong winds may blow almost 60 miles per hour faster than the hurricane's average speed, causing localized pockets of severe damage.

Link-ups

RADAR BULLETS

After the end of a war, land mines often continue to be a terrible hazard to soldiers and civilians alike. Usually they can be found only by a time-consuming and dangerous search of the ground. However, a new system can map the location of hidden mines quickly and accurately by firing radar bullets from a helicopter. As the bullet hits the ground it sends a radar map of its surroundings back to the helicopter.

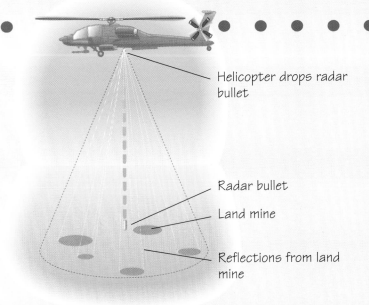

Helicopter drops radar bullet

Radar bullet

Land mine

Reflections from land mine

TRANSPONDERS

TRANSPONDERS ARE USEFUL RADIO DEVICES THAT DO NOTHING UNTIL THEY RECEIVE A CERTAIN RADIO SIGNAL. WHEN THE CORRECT SIGNAL ARRIVES, THE TRANSPONDER BURSTS INTO LIFE AND STARTS TRANSMITTING. TRANSPONDERS ARE ALREADY STANDARD ON AIRCRAFT, BUT IN THE FUTURE THEY WILL BE USED MUCH MORE WIDELY.

In aviation, radar does a lot more than just locate aircraft. A second radar system carried by airliners and, increasingly, ships, uses radio waves to trigger a transmitter in the plane that sends out information about the plane and where it is going. The device in the plane is a transmitter-responder, or transponder. In the future, transponders will be used in other ways. A transponder in a family car or a truck could locate the vehicle if it is stolen. And micro-transponders are already sometimes implanted in pets, to help find them if they run away.

Transponders locate and identify airliners. Future cars, buses, trucks, and even people may be provided with transponders.

HUMAN TRANSPONDER

On August 24, 1998, Professor Kevin Warwick, professor of Cybernetics at Reading University in England, had a transponder implanted in his forearm—a world first. The transponder is $\frac{7}{8}$ inch long and $\frac{1}{8}$ inch across. When a radio signal is transmitted to it, a coil inside the transponder generates an electric current. This powers a transmitter, which sends out a unique 64-bit code. By placing detectors around the university, Professor Warwick's secretary now knows where he is all the time! This experiment shows what could be done with transponders. If everyone in a company had a transponder implant, the system could be programmed to recognize each individual transponder code. The transponder could also be used to automatically activate lights, heating, and other equipment when someone entered a room.

BUSES ON THE WEB

In an experiment in France, buses have been equipped with transponders and Global Positioning System (GPS) receivers. The GPS receivers give the positions of buses as they move around town, and these positions are superimposed onto a computer-generated street map. This information is put onto the World Wide Web. By calling up the web site and clicking on any bus, information about that particular bus is transmitted by its transponder. A menu of information, from its route and when it was last serviced to the name of its driver, appears on the screen. This helps the company to analyze the speed and movements of its buses, and to adjust the numbers and timings of buses accordingly. Freight companies can keep track of their trucks in the same way.

STAYING IN CONTROL

In another technological advance, every piece of office machinery and every household appliance could soon have its own built-in radio transmitter and receiver for two-way wireless communication. Forgot to switch off the oven before you left home? Just call it on your mobile phone and turn it off. The German electronics company Siemens has already built a house in which the appliances and equipment can be voice controlled from inside, and by mobile phone from anywhere else.

History links

FRIEND OR FOE?

Radar has made it possible to detect aircraft long before they come within sight. But, at first, there was no way of telling if they were friendly aircraft. In the chaos of war, pilots and ground radar stations have to be able to identify enemy aircraft as soon as they are detected. A system called Identification Friend or Foe was developed to solve this problem. Transponders in the aircraft allow them to be recognized electronically.

Link-ups

SHIP CODES

A new radio system for shipping, called the Global Maritime Distress and Safety System, will use transponders to send out a ship's identity and position automatically in the event of an emergency. Every ship will have a unique nine-digit code. Any ship will be able to telephone any other ship by dialing its code number.

BIG BROTHER

WATCH OUT! BIG BROTHER IS LOOKING AND LISTENING! GOODS, ANIMALS, AND PEOPLE CAN BE MONITORED BY ELECTRONIC BUGS WHICH EITHER TRANSMIT INFORMATION CONTINUOUSLY OR REVEAL THEIR IDENTITY ONLY WHEN THEY ARE SCANNED BY RADIO WAVES.

Technology that was once available only to James Bond is now becoming much more commonplace in our everyday lives. Anyone thinking of committing a crime should think again—someone or something could be watching. CCTV cameras capture the activities of shoplifters and bank robbers on video tape. Criminals are so aware of video surveillance that many shops and offices have two video security systems—one that criminals can easily find and disable, and another, hidden system that records their activities.

STORE SECURITY

One branch of the security industry deals with Electronic Article Surveillance (EAS) – protecting goods in stores. Clothes, books, CDs, and hundreds of other items are often protected by electronic tags. If an item that has not been paid for is carried out through any exit, a detector sounds an alarm.

The future of EAS is SmartEAS – smart tags containing chips that can be programmed with information about the product to which they are attached. SmartEAS tags can be used to track a product all the way from the manufacturer to the final customer, which is very useful in the war against counterfeit goods. Most products are identified by barcodes. These codes are read individually by scanning each one with a laser. A SmartEAS reader can scan 40 tags a second by radio. Inventories that take hours today will be done in seconds with SmartEAS.

Smile, you may be on TV! Modern spy cameras are so small that they can be hidden almost anywhere.

TRACKING PETS

A tracking system for pet animals works in a similar way to SmartEAS. A tiny chip is implanted under the animal's skin, usually at the back of the neck. When a low-power radio signal from a handheld scanner is received by the implant, it sends back a unique number that identifies the animal. Valuable wild animals are sometimes identified in the same way, especially if they are part of a breeding program, or if they are being released into the wild and need to be monitored again from time to time.

HELP! I'VE BEEN STOLEN!

Vehicle theft is such a serious problem that cars and trucks are now being bugged by their owners so that they can be found if they are stolen. The vehicle is fitted with a Global Positioning System (GPS) receiver. The GPS can work out where the car is by using radio signals

Electronic tags are used to protect goods in stores from being stolen.

History links

VIDEO EVIDENCE

In 1981, the police received a tip-off that a security van carrying £800,000 was to be robbed in London. The police recorded the robbery on videotape before arresting the gang. The recording was shown to the jury at the robbers' trial at the Old Bailey. It was one of the first trials where video evidence helped to secure a conviction.

Link-ups

GPS

The Global Positioning System (GPS) was set up as a military system for locating warships, fighters, bombers, tanks, and individual soldiers. Today, anyone can buy and use a GPS receiver.

from orbiting satellites. This information is transmitted to a control center where the vehicle's position is superimposed on a street map. If the vehicle is reported stolen, or if its alarm system is triggered, its position flashes up on the control room screen. The hidden bug enables the police to go straight to the vehicle.

Bugs are not always used for security or crime detection. General Motors' On-Star system can unlock the car doors if the owner locks the keys inside or flash the headlights if the owner loses the vehicle in a parking lot. It also calls the emergency services if the airbag is deployed. A central control room keeps in touch with the car and controls things such as the locks and lights by using the car's cellular telephone to communicate with its electrical systems.

ANIMAL TRACKS

PEOPLE CAN TRACK ANIMALS ON LAND AND IN THE OCEANS BY ATTACHING RADIO TRANSMITTERS TO THEM. TAGGING CREATURES MAY REVEAL WHERE THEY GO TO FEED, TO MATE, OR TO HIBERNATE. IT EVEN PERMITS SCIENTISTS TO STUDY THE EFFECTS OF GLOBAL WARMING ON SOME SPECIES.

The Earth's climate is changing. It may be warming up because of a natural change or, as many scientists believe, because of the "greenhouse effect" caused by human activities. Global warming means that ice near the two poles melts earlier each year. This change is affecting the feeding and breeding cycles of creatures that live in these regions.

POLAR TRACKING

Polar bears live by hunting seals on the vast expanses of ice that surround the North Pole. When the ice recedes in the spring, the bears come ashore in northern Canada. However, polar bears find very little to eat on land. They may lose half their body weight while they wait for the sea to freeze. Then they can hunt seals under the ice again. If the ice melts early, the bears don't have enough time to build up the body fat necessary to keep them going on land. They produce fewer, smaller cubs which are less able to survive than normal fit and healthy cubs.

Every year, scientists go out onto the polar ice and seek out these animals to monitor their progress. A few individuals are fitted with radio transmitting collars, so that they can be found by helicopter or tracked by satellite. The collars are also being used to discover where pregnant female bears go to give birth to their cubs—to settle the question of whether they choose a new place for each birth, or return to the same place each time.

Radio collars allow scientists to track polar bears in Canada so that they can learn more about the bears' movements and habits.

BRINGING BEAVERS BACK

As towns and cities grow, and the roads that link them spread out across the countryside, animals that avoid human contact are forced to retreat farther and farther. Sometimes, if their habitats or the plants and creatures on which they feed become scarce, they may disappear from an area altogether. In some places, animals are being re-introduced into areas where they once lived. Radio tags are sometimes fitted to these animals to provide scientists with vital information.

Beavers once lived in Scotland, but they have long since died out. However, European beavers are about to be released again into the wild in Scotland. The experiment has attracted opposition from forest rangers and fish farmers, who fear that the beavers may damage their trees and fish. So, the animals will be fitted with radio tags to check where they go. If they head for a nearby forest and damage trees, or swim out to the nearest fish farm and take fish, the radio tags will make it possible to find, trap, and remove the animals from the area once more.

Radio collars attached to animals are usually designed with a biodegradable link so that they fall off after a time—just in case the animal can't be found again to have the collar removed.

History links

TAGGING FISH

In 1985, researchers wanted to know more about how salmon migrate along the Snake and Columbia rivers in Washington. They implanted some of the young fish with electronic tags that were detected as they passed through hydroelectric projects on the rivers.

NATURE'S RADIO STATIONS

HUMANS HAVE BEEN SENDING RADIO SIGNALS TO ONE ANOTHER FOR MORE THAN 100 YEARS, BUT RADIO WAVES HAVE BEEN CROSSING SPACE FOR COUNTLESS MILLIONS OF YEARS. RADIO ASTRONOMERS USE THE WAVES THAT POUR OUT OF STARS AND GALAXIES TO LEARN MORE ABOUT THE UNIVERSE.

	Carbon monoxide	Ammonia		Formaldehyde		Hydroxyl
mm	2.6	12.6		62		180
	3.4	13.5				
		Water				
	Hydrogen cyanide					

This diagram shows the wavelengths of several natural radio transmitters.

Radio astronomy is the branch of science that deals with natural radio signals from space. Astronomers use telescopes to study these natural radio signals. Most radio telescopes have a giant metal dish to collect as much radio energy as possible and reflect it onto a receiver. Chemical elements and compounds in space each give out different radio signals. For example, hydrogen, the most abundant element in the universe, sends out radio waves with a wavelength of 211 millimeters. Astronomers can identify what something is made from by tuning in to the radio signal it sends out, just like tuning in to a radio station.

When you look at a galaxy, most of the matter you are looking at is hydrogen. Astronomers often find that the hydrogen on one side of the galaxy transmits signals with a shorter wavelength than normal, while the hydrogen on the other side of the galaxy transmits signals with a longer wavelength. That's because the galaxy is spinning. Measuring the lengths of the radio waves tells astronomers how fast and in which direction a galaxy is whirling.

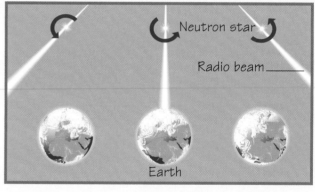

We receive a burst of radio energy every time the radio beam from a spinning pulsar sweeps across the Earth.

PULSATING STARS

A large star ends its days by exploding, blasting its outer layers out into space and leaving a tiny core called a neutron star. This strange star spins rapidly, up to a thousand times a second, and sends out jets of radio energy from its poles. If it wobbles on its axis, the radio jets sometimes sweep across the Earth and the star appears to be blinking on and off. Radio astronomers can tune into the signals coming from these pulsating stars, or pulsars. The speed of the bleeping signal from pulsars shows how fast they are spinning.

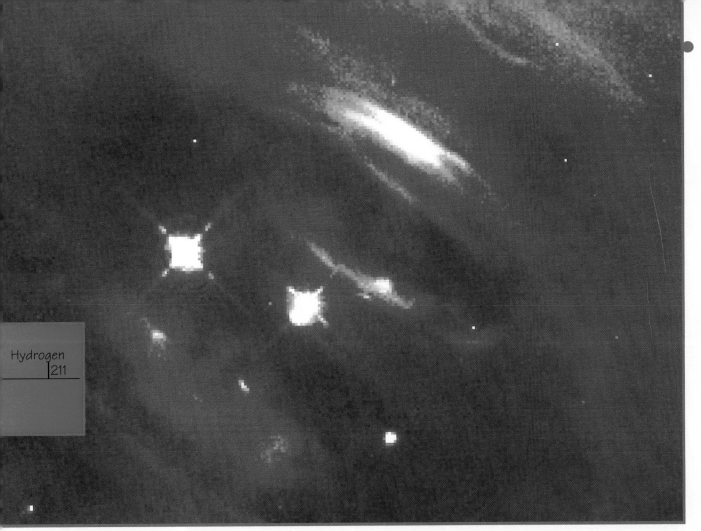

Hydrogen
211

SPACE NOISE

Instead of picking up faint radio signals from distant stars and galaxies, radio telescopes can sometimes be swamped by stronger signals from satellites orbiting the Earth. It's like trying to hear someone whispering in the middle of a cheering football crowd. For example, a hydrogen atom joined to an oxygen atom, called a hydroxyl radical, sends out a radio signal with a wavelength of 180 millimeters. But this signal can be difficult to detect because, unfortunately, some mobile telephone satellites transmit using the same wavelength. Astronomers are hoping that the new mobile telephone satellite operators will agree to keep important radio wavelengths free for astronomical observations—for at least part of the day, if not permanently. If the space around Earth becomes too noisy with radio signals from satellites, radio telescopes may have to be set up in a place where satellites won't interfere with them—on the far side of the Moon, perhaps.

A rapidly spinning pulsar at the center of the Crab Nebula is all that remains of a star that exploded as a supernova in 1054. The explosion was so bright that it was clearly visible from Earth.

History links

RADIO ASTRONOMY

Radio astronomy was invented by accident. In 1931, the Bell Telephone Laboratories asked an engineer named Karl Jansky to investigate the hissing noise that interfered with ship-to-shore radio communications. Jansky discovered that it came from space, in the direction of the center of the Milky Way galaxy. An American radio engineer, Grote Reber, read about Jansky's discovery and, by 1937, he had built a dish antenna. He used his dish to search the sky for radio signals. For the next ten years, he was the world's only radio astronomer.

TIME LINE

WORLD DATES

1873   James Clerk Maxwell predicts the existence of radio waves.

1883   George Francis Fitzgerald suggests how radio waves might be made.

         The volcanic island Krakatoa explodes, making the loudest bang ever heard on Earth.

1885   Karl Benz builds the first gasoline-engine motor car.

1888   Heinrich Hertz produces and detects radio waves for the first time.

1894   Guglielmo Marconi invents radio communication, also called wireless telegraphy.

1897   Ferdinand Braun makes the first cathode ray tube, a device that is essential to the invention of electronic television.

1898   Nikola Tesla shows how to control model ships by radio in Madison Square Garden, New York.

1903   Orville Wright makes the first sustained powered flight.

1904   Reginald Aubrey Fessenden demonstrates the transmission of speech by radio.

1906   The first radio broadcasts of sounds other than Morse Code are made—music and the spoken word.

        Arthur Korn transmits television pictures 1,000 miles using telephone wires.

1909   Guglielmo Marconi and Karl Ferdinand Braun win the Nobel Prize for Physics for inventing wireless telegraphy.

        Louis Blériot makes the first airplane flight across the English Channel

1910   A radio message from the ship *Montrose* informs police that the murderer Dr. Crippen is on board, leading to Crippen's arrest.

1912   The passenger liner *Titanic* strikes an iceberg and sinks in the North Atlantic Ocean.

1914-18 World War I.

1915   The first transatlantic radio telephone call is made between the United States and France.

1919   Short-wave radio is developed.

1920   The first regular radio broadcasts from a licensed radio station begin in Pittsburgh, Pennsylvania.

1923   Vladimir Zworykin invents the electronic television camera.

1924   The first portable radio goes on sale in the United States.

1925   John Logie Baird produces the first television picture.

1926   John Logie Baird invents television broadcasting.

        Robert Goddard launches the first liquid fuel rocket.

1927   John Logie Baird invents the video disk.

        Charles Lindbergh makes the first non-stop solo flight across the Atlantic Ocean.

1928   John Logie Baird demonstrates color television.

      Radio beacons are used for the first time for navigation.

      Television broadcasts begin in the United States.

1929   Bell Laboratories develop an electronic color television system.

1930   The planet Pluto is discovered by Clyde Tombaugh.

        Nylon is invented by Wallace Carruthers at the Du Pont chemical company.

        Frank Whittle invents the jet engine.

1932   Karl Jansky builds the first radio telescope.

      The car radio is invented by Blaupunkt.

RADIO AND TELEVISION DATES

WORLD DATES

1935   Radar is invented by a team of British scientists led by Robert Watson-Watt.

The *Hindenburg* airship crashes to the ground.

1936   The BBC (British Broadcasting Corporation) begins regular television broadcasts.

1939-45   World War II.

1947   Charles "Chuck" Yeager makes the first supersonic flight in the experimental rocket-plane, the *Bell* X-1.

1953   Edmund Hillary and Tenzing Norgay climb the world's tallest mountain, Mount Everest, for the first time. The structure of DNA is discovered by James Watson and Francis Crick.

1954   The first transistor radio is made by Regency Electronics.

1957   The world's first artificial satellite is launched by the Soviet Union.

1960   The first passive communications satellite, Echo 1, is launched. The first navigational satellite, Transit 1B, is launched.

1961   Cosmonaut Yuri Gagarin becomes the first human being to orbit the Earth.

1962   The first active communications satellite, Telstar, is launched.

1965   The first commercial communications satellite, Early Bird (Intelsat 1), is launched. Passenger planes land automatically for the first time, using radio signals transmitted by beacons on the ground.

1967   The first satellite navigation system, called Transit, is established by the US Navy.

Christiann Barnard performs the first heart transplant.

1969   The first human being walks on the Moon, Apollo 11 astronaut Neil Armstrong.

1970   The Pentagon begins development of the Global Positioning System (GPS) satellite navigation system.

The first Jumbo Jet enters service.

1971   The first Intel microprocessor is introduced. The first space station, Salyut 1, is launched.

1973   Supermarket barcodes are introduced. The *Skylab* space station is launched.

1976   The supersonic airliner Concorde enters service.

1978   The first test tube baby, Louise Brown, is born.

1980   The wreck of the passenger liner *Titanic* is discovered,

1981   The Space Shuttle is launched for the first time.

1983   Satellite television broadcasts direct to people's homes begin in Indianapolis.

1986   The *Mir* space station is launched. The nuclear reactor at Chernobyl explodes.

1987   The world's five billionth person is born.

1990   Nelson Mandela is released from prison in South Africa.

1991   Airliners are furnished with satelite telephones.

1997   Andy Green sets the first supersonic land speed record in Thrust SSC.

1999   The world's six billionth person is born

GLOSSARY

AMPLITUDE MODULATION (AM) A method for sending information by radio. The information modulates (changes) the amplitude (size) of a carrier wave.

ANALOG A system that transmits information as changes in the frequency (number) or amplitude (size) of an electrical signal or radio waves.

ANTENNA The part of a radio or television system that transmits or receives radio signals.

ATMOSPHERE The gases that surround Earth (or any other planet, moon, or star).

BROADCASTING Transmitting radio or television programs over a wide area so that anyone with an antenna and radio or TV set can receive them.

CABLE TELEVISION A television service delivered to the home by optical or metal cables.

CARRIER WAVE A radio wave that is combined with an information signal, such as a radio or television program, so that it carries the information from a transmitter to a receiving antenna.

CATHODE A negative electrode in an electrical circuit.

CATHODE RAY A stream of electrons produced by a cathode.

CATHODE RAY TUBE A glass tube in which cathode rays hit a phosphor-coated screen at the front of the tube to produce a glowing symbol or picture. A television screen is the front of a cathode ray tube.

CHANNEL A band of radio frequencies used to carry a broadcast or voice communication. Each radio and television station is broadcast on a different channel.

CLOSED CIRCUIT TELEVISION (CCTV) A television system in which pictures from video cameras are fed directly to one or more video screens.

COMPACT DISK READ-ONLY MEMORY (CD-ROM) A CD that holds computer data.

CORDLESS TELEPHONE A telephone whose handset communicates with the rest of the telephone by low-power radio signals instead of a length of cable.

DATA COMPRESSION A technique for reducing the number of bits of information that have to be transmitted.

DIGITAL Made up of digits, or pulses.

DIGITAL VERSATILE DISK (DVD) A laser disk the same size as a CD, but a DVD is able to store high-quality audio and video (sound and pictures).

DIGITAL VERSATILE DISK READ ONLY MEMORY (DVD-ROM) A type of DVD that can store computer data.

DIRECT BROADCAST BY SATELLITE (DBS) Transmitting television and radio programs from satellites directly into individual homes.

DOWNLINK The radio signal that is transmitted from an orbiting satellite down to a receiver on Earth.

ELECTRODE An electrical contact where electricity enters or leaves a circuit or part of a circuit.

ELECTROMAGNETIC SPECTRUM The whole range of electromagnetic (combined electric and magnetic) waves, from radio waves thousands of miles long to gamma rays a fraction of a millimeter long.

ELECTRON A particle of matter with a negative electrical charge, found in all atoms.

FIBER OPTIC CABLE A cable made from optical fibres, using laser beams to carry information.

FREQUENCY The number of waves of an electrical signal or radio signal that passes any point in a second. Frequency is measured in hertz. One hertz is one complete wave, or cycle, per second.

FREQUENCY MODULATION (FM) A method for sending information by radio. The information modulates (changes) the frequency of a carrier wave.

GIGABYTE One billion bytes of digital information. Each byte is eight bits long. Each bit is a zero or one.

GIGAHERTZ One billion hertz (cycles, or waves, per second).

HIGH DEFINITION TELEVISION (HDTV) Any of the new television systems that offer very high-quality television pictures.

HERTZ (Hz) One cycle, or wave, per second, named after the scientist Heinrich Hertz.

IN-CAR ENTERTAINMENT (ICE) The radio, cassette, and CD equipment designed for use in cars.

INFRARED Invisible electromagnetic waves from a thousandth of a millimeter to a millimeter long, between the red end of the rainbow and radio waves.

INTERACTIVE Involving two-way communication between a person and an electronic system.

IONOSPHERE A band of electrically charged particles high in the Earth's atmosphere that reflect radio waves longer than about 100 feet.

IONS Electrically charged particles produced when atoms gain or lose electrons.

LASER A device that produces an intense beam of light.

MEGABYTE One million bytes of computer data. Each byte is eight bits long. A bit is a binary digit—a zero or one.

MEGAHERTZ One million cycles, or waves, per second.

MICROPHONE A device that changes sound waves into an electric current.

MOBILE TELEPHONE A telephone that is linked to the rest of the international telephone network by radio. It is also called a cellular telephone.

NEURAL NET A type of computer that can process different pieces of information at the same time, in a way similar to the human brain.

OPTICAL FIBER A hair-thin strand of glass used to carry information as laser beams.

PAY-PER-VIEW A way to receive special programs such as movies or sports events by paying for each program.

PHOSPHOR A chemical used on the back of a television screen that glows when electrons hit it. A television picture is built up from three different phosphors that glow red, green, or blue.

RADAR A system that uses radio waves to locate far-away objects such as planes and ships.

RADIO The use of electromagnetic waves between about a millimeter long and thousands of miles long for communications and broadcasting.

RADIO MICROPHONE A microphone that is linked to the rest of a sound recording or transmission system by radio.

RADIO TELESCOPE A telescope that makes maps and pictures of distant stars and galaxies from the radio energy they send out.

RADIO WINDOW The band of radio wavelengths between about one inch and 100 feet long that can pass through Earth's atmosphere. All other wavelengths are either reflected or absorbed by the atmosphere.

SAMPLING A method for digitizing an analog wave—that is, changing a varying electric current into a series of electrical pulses.

SATELLITE DISH A metal bowl that focuses radio waves onto a receiver held above the bowl. A satellite dish can also work in reverse, reflecting radio waves from a transmitter above the bowl to form a narrow beam.

SENSOR A device that senses, or responds to, something in its surroundings such as temperature, pressure, or sound and changes it into an electric current.

SIGNAL An electric current or group of radio waves that carry information.

TELECOMMUNICATION Passing information from one person to another over a long distance by cable or radio waves.

TELEMETRY Taking measurements at a distance using sensors. The measurements are sent back by cable or radio.

TERRESTRIAL On Earth. Terrestrial television is a television service broadcast from radio transmitters on Earth.

TRANSPONDER A radio device that transmits only when it receives a particular radio signal.

UPLINK The radio signal that is transmitted from the Earth up to a satellite.

VIDEO Transmitting, receiving, or recording television pictures.

WATT An amount of electrical power that shows how quickly electricity is changed into other forms of energy such as heat or light.

WAVELENGTH The length of a radio wave.

FURTHER READING

Balcziak, Bill. *Radio*, "Communication Today and Tomorrow" series. Vero Beach, FL: Rourke Enterprises, Inc., 1989.

Gaines, Ann. *Satellite Communications*, "Making Contact" series. Mankato, MN: Smart Apple Media, 1999.

Gibson, Diane. *Television*, "Making Contact" series. Mankato, MN: Smart Apple Media, 1999.

Hoare, Stephen. *The Digital Revolution*, "Twentieth Century Inventions" series. Austin, TX: Raintree Steck-Vaughn Publishers, 1999.

Lafferty, Peter. *Radio and Television*, "Worldwise" series. Danbury, CT: Watts, 1998.

Internet links

- You can find out more about some of the subjects in this book by looking at the following web sites:

- www.mtr.org
  (The American Museum of Television and Radio)

- www.atek.com/satellite
  (Satellites and how they work)

- www.alcatel.com/telecom/space/systems/worldspace/index.htm
  (Digital satellite radio)

- www.onstar.com
  (The General Motors system for communicating with cars)

- www.newscientist.com
  (*New Scientist* – searchable articles)

- www.sciam.com
  (*Scientific American* – searchable articles)

- www.track-it.com
  (Telemetry using radio collars)

- www.cntower.ca
  (All about the CN Tower)

- www.vbs.bt.co.uk/bt_bs/btt_tour.htm
  (All about the BT Tower)

- rapidttp.co.za/transponder
  (No 'www' prefix)
  (All about transponders)

- www.ai.mit.edu/projects/kismet/kismet.html
  (All about the Kismet robot)

- www.jasonproject.org
  (All about the Jason Project)